Echoes of the Forsaken

by

Adriano Alamia

Table of Contents

Chapter 1

The Break-In

The night air was thick with the scent of rain-soaked earth and blooming jasmine, a deceptive calm cloaking the sinister events about to unfold. The old mansion on the edge of town, draped in ivy and shadows, stood silent under the pale moonlight. Inside, an elderly woman named Eleanora sat in her parlor, her gnarled hands caressing the ancient, leather-bound tome in her lap.

Eleanora's daughter, Claire, had left for a business trip earlier that week, leaving her mother alone in the sprawling estate. Eleanora had assured her daughter that she would be fine, but Claire had felt a nagging sense of unease as she drove away. Eleanora had lived in the mansion for decades, a relic of a bygone era, filled with memories and secrets.

As the clock struck midnight, three figures crept through the dense underbrush, their dark clothing blending seamlessly with the night. Lucas, the leader, moved with calculated precision, his eyes never straying from the mansion's dimly lit windows. Behind him, Trey and Mark followed, their breaths shallow and hearts pounding in anticipation.

"Remember," Lucas whispered, his voice barely audibles over the rustling leaves. "In and out, quick and quiet. We take everything of value and we're gone before anyone notices."

The three men approached the back door, their gloved hands working swiftly to pick the lock. The door swung open with a soft creak, and they slipped inside, their eyes adjusting to the dim interior. The scent of lavender and old books filled their nostrils, a stark contrast to the musty air outside.

Lucas signaled for Trey and Mark to split up and search the house. They moved silently, like shadows, each taking a different direction. Lucas made his way towards the kitchen, his eyes scanning for anything of value. Trey headed upstairs; his steps cautious on the creaking floorboards. Mark, the youngest and most nervous of the trio, lingered in the hallway, his heart racing with every sound.

As he searched the kitchen, Lucas couldn't shake the feeling of unease that had settled over him. The house was too quiet, too still. He pocketed a silver candlestick and some antique spoons, his mind racing with thoughts of what they might find. Jewelry, cash, perhaps even hidden treasures. But the silence was unnerving.

Upstairs, Trey moved from room to room, his flashlight casting eerie shadows on the walls.

He pocketed a few pieces of jewelry and some old coins, but his attention was drawn to a door at the end of the hallway. It was slightly ajar, and a faint light glowed from within. He approached cautiously, his heart pounding in his chest.

As he pushed the door open, he found himself in a small, cluttered study. Books lined the walls, and an old desk sat in the center of the room, papers and trinkets scattered across its surface. But it was the painting above the desk that caught his eye. It depicted a beautiful young woman with piercing blue eyes and a serene expression. Trey felt a chill run down his spine as he realized the woman in the painting bore a striking resemblance to the old woman downstairs.

Mark, meanwhile, had made his way to the parlor. He hesitated outside the door, listening to the faint sound of a woman's voice. It was Eleanora, her voice soft and melodic, as if she were reciting a poem or a prayer. Mark took a deep breath and pushed the door open, stepping into the room.

Eleanora sat in an armchair; her eyes fixed on the pages of her book. The room was dimly lit by a single lamp, casting long shadows on the walls. The air was thick with the scent of lavender and something else, something ancient and powerful. Mark felt a sudden urge to run, but he forced himself to stay calm.

"You shouldn't be here," Eleanora said softly, her voice carrying an otherworldly resonance.

Mark froze, his heart pounding in his chest. "We're just here for the valuables, lady. Hand them over and no one gets hurt," he said, trying to sound confident.

Eleanora looked up, her piercing blue eyes seeming to see straight through him. She smiled, a slow, chilling smile that sent shivers down his spine. "You have no idea what you've walked into," she whispered.

Before Mark could react, Eleanora raised her hands, the air around her shimmering with a golden light. She spoke in a language he didn't recognize, her voice growing louder and more powerful with each word. The room seemed to shrink, the walls closing in around him.

Upstairs, Trey felt the house tremble. He rushed back to the hallway, calling for Lucas. Lucas, hearing the commotion, abandoned his search and ran towards the stairs. But as they reached the parlor, an invisible force threw them back, slamming them against the walls. The door they had entered through was now a solid wall, the room sealing itself off from the rest of the house.

"What the hell is happening?" Trey screamed, panic rising in his chest.

Eleanora stood, her form towering over them, her eyes glowing with an eerie light. "You are trapped," she said, her voice echoing in their minds. "You will pay for your greed and trespass."

The air grew thick with the scent of decay and sulfur, the once beautiful mansion transforming into a labyrinth of horrors. Whispers filled the air, voices of long-dead souls echoing through the halls. Shadows moved on their own, creeping ever closer to the terrified men.

Lucas, Trey, and Mark found themselves trapped in a nightmare. The house seemed to have a life of its own, its walls shifting and changing, leading them in endless circles. Eleanora appeared and disappeared at will, her presence a constant reminder of their impending doom.

Days turned into weeks, and the men grew weaker with each passing day. Food and water appeared and disappeared at random, their minds unraveling from the constant fear and isolation. They were driven to the brink of madness, their only hope of escape lying in the dark magic of the witch.

And so, the three men remained trapped in the house of secrets, their fate sealed by the powerful witch who had ensnared them. They would never escape, forever haunted by the shadows and whispers of the mansion.

But Eleanora had not finished with them yet. She had plans for these intruders, plans that would stretch far beyond the confines of her home. For the shadows always seek balance, and the men would soon learn that their true torment had only just begun.

Lucas, Trey, and Mark sat huddled in the parlor, the weight of their situation pressing down on them like a physical force. The once-grand room now felt like a prison, its walls closing in around them. They had been trapped in the mansion for what felt like an eternity, their minds and bodies battered by the relentless torment of the house.

As the days turned into weeks, the men found themselves reflecting on their pasts, their mistakes, and the choices that had led them to this point. They had come to the mansion seeking fortune, but they had found only despair.

Lucas, the leader of the group, had always been driven by ambition. Growing up in a poor neighborhood, he had learned early on that the world was a harsh place, and he had vowed to do whatever it took to rise above his circumstances. He had built a reputation as a cunning and resourceful thief, always one step ahead of the law. But his ambition had also made him reckless, leading him to take greater and greater risks. The mansion was supposed to be his biggest score yet, the job that would set him up for life. But now, as he sat in the darkened parlor, he wondered if he had finally gone too far.

Trey, Lucas's right-hand man, had a more complicated past. He had grown up in a loving family, but a series of bad choices had led him down a dark path. He had fallen in with the wrong crowd, started using drugs, and eventually turned to crime to support his habit. Lucas had taken him under his wing, offering him a way out of the cycle of addiction and desperation. Trey had seen the mansion job as a chance to make a clean break, to start over. But now, as the shadows closed in around him, he realized that his past was not so easily escaped.

Mark, the youngest and most inexperienced of the group, had joined Lucas and Trey out of a sense of loyalty and a desire for adventure. He had grown up idolizing his older brother, who had been a part of Lucas's crew before he was killed in a botched robbery. Mark had wanted to prove himself, to show that he could be just as brave and resourceful as his brother. But now, as he cowered in the darkened room, he felt only fear and regret.

As the men sat in silence, the air grew thick with the scent of decay and sulfur. The shadows in the room seemed to move with a life of their own, creeping ever closer. Whispers filled the air, voices of long-dead souls echoing through the halls.

And then, the door to the parlor creaked open, and Eleanora stepped inside. Her eyes glowed with an eerie light, and her presence filled the room with a sense of foreboding.

"You have learned your lesson," she said, her voice a haunting melody. "But your journey is far from over. The house demands a sacrifice, and it will not rest until it has claimed what it is owed."

The men exchanged fearful glances, their hearts pounding in their chests. They knew that they had no choice but to face whatever horrors awaited them. The house would not let them go without a fight.

Chapter 3
Shadows of the Past

The days passed in a blur of fear and confusion. The men tried to make sense of their situation, to find a way out of the house's grip. They explored every corner of the mansion, searching for clues, for anything that might help them escape. But the house seemed to conspire against them, its labyrinthine corridors and shifting walls leading them in endless circles.

One evening, as the sun set and the shadows lengthened, Lucas stumbled upon a small, forgotten room at the back of the mansion. It was filled with old books, dusty artifacts, and strange, arcane symbols. In the center of the room was a large, ornate mirror, its surface tarnished and cracked.

Lucas approached the mirror cautiously, his heart pounding in his chest. He reached out a hand, brushing the dust from its surface. As he did, the mirror seemed to come to life, its surface rippling like water.

"Help me," a voice whispered, faint and distant. Lucas recoiled, his eyes widening in shock. He peered into the mirror, and for a moment, he thought he saw a face, a pair of eyes staring back at him.

The voice came again, stronger this time. "Help me... and I can help you."

Lucas swallowed hard, his mind racing. Was this another trick of the house, another way to torment them? Or was it a genuine plea for help? He took a deep breath, steeling himself.

"Who are you?" he asked, his voice trembling.

The mirror's surface shimmered, and the voice replied, "I am bound to this house, just as you are. But I know its secrets, its weaknesses. Help me break free, and I will help you escape."

Lucas felt a flicker of hope, a glimmer of light in the darkness. "How?" he asked, desperate for answers.

The voice hesitated, then spoke again. "There is a ritual, a way to break the house's hold. But it requires great sacrifice, and the help of the witch who binds us all."

Lucas's heart sank. Eleanora. Convincing her to help them would be nearly impossible. But he knew he had to try. It was their only hope.

Lucas returned to the parlor, his mind racing with the possibilities. Trey and Mark looked up as he entered, their faces etched with worry and exhaustion.

"I found something," Lucas said, his voice low. "A way out. But it won't be easy."

Trey and Mark listened intently as Lucas explained what he had discovered. The mirror, the voice, the ritual. They knew it was a long shot, but it was the only lead they had.

"We need Eleanora's help," Lucas concluded. "We have to convince her to perform the ritual."

Trey frowned. "And why would she do that? She has no reason to help us."

"Maybe not," Lucas admitted. "But we have to try. If we can convince her that it will benefit her in some way, maybe she'll agree."

The three men spent the next few days watching Eleanora, trying to find a way to approach her. They observed her rituals, her interactions with the house, and slowly, they began to piece together a plan.

One evening, as the shadows deepened and the air grew thick with the scent of lavender and sage, Lucas approached Eleanora. She was in the parlor, reading from her ancient tome, her eyes glowing with a soft, ethereal light.

"Eleanora," Lucas said, his voice steady. "We need to talk."

The witch looked up, her gaze piercing. "What is it, Lucas? Have you finally accepted your fate?"

"No," Lucas replied. "But I think we can help each other."

Eleanora's eyes narrowed. "And what makes you think I need your help?"

Lucas took a deep breath. "I found a mirror, in one of the rooms. There's a voice trapped inside, someone who claims to know how to break the house's hold. But we need your help to perform the ritual."

Eleanora's expression softened, just a fraction. "A mirror, you say? And a voice?"

"Yes," Lucas said. "The voice said it knows the house's secrets, its weaknesses. If we can free it, it will help us escape."

Eleanora was silent for a long moment, her eyes distant. Finally, she spoke. "Very well, Lucas. I will help you. But know this: the ritual is dangerous, and the cost will be great. Are you willing to pay the price?"

Lucas nodded, determination in his eyes. "We have no choice. We have to try."

Eleanora closed her book and stood, her form towering over them. "Then let us begin."

Chapter 4
The Bargain

The air grew heavy with anticipation as Eleanora led the men to the small, forgotten room at the back of the mansion. The mirror stood in the center, its surface shimmering with a faint, otherworldly light.

Eleanora began to prepare for the ritual, her movements precise and deliberate. She drew intricate symbols on the floor with chalk, lit candles, and placed strange, arcane artifacts around the room. The scent of burning incense filled the air, mingling with the lavender and sage.

Lucas, Trey, and Mark watched in silence, their hearts pounding with a mix of fear and hope. They knew the stakes were high, and the outcome uncertain, but they were determined to see it through.

Eleanora stood before the mirror, her eyes closed, her hands raised. She began to chant, her voice low and melodic, the ancient words resonating through the room. The mirror's surface rippled, and the voice emerged, stronger than before.

"Thank you," the voice said, its tone filled with relief and gratitude. "You have freed me from my prison. Now, I will help you escape."

Eleanora's chant grew louder, the symbols on the floor glowing with a soft, golden light. The air crackled with energy, the room filled with a sense of anticipation and power.

"Now," Eleanora said, her voice commanding. "Speak the name of the one you wish to sacrifice."

Lucas hesitated, his mind racing. He knew the cost would be great, but he had no other choice. He closed his eyes, took a deep breath, and spoke the name.

"Mark."

Mark's eyes widened in shock and betrayal. "What? No! You can't do this!"

"I'm sorry, Mark," Lucas said, his voice filled with regret. "But we have no other choice. The house demands a sacrifice, and you..."

Eleanora's chant grew louder, the energy in the room reaching a fever pitch. The mirror's surface shimmered, and a blinding light filled the room. Mark screamed, his voice echoing through the halls as he was consumed by the ritual.

And then, it was over. The light faded, and the room fell silent. The mirror's surface was smooth and clear, the voice gone. Mark was nowhere to be seen.

Eleanora turned to Lucas and Trey, her eyes filled with a mixture of sorrow and satisfaction. "The ritual is complete," she said. "You are free."

Lucas and Trey stood in stunned silence, the reality of what had just happened sinking in. They had escaped, but at a terrible cost. Mark was gone, sacrificed to the house's insatiable hunger.

Eleanora watched them, her expression unreadable. "You have paid the price," she said softly. "But remember, the shadows always seek balance. The house will not rest until it has claimed its due."

Lucas and Trey nodded, their faces pale and drawn. They knew that their ordeal was far from over, that the house would continue to haunt them, even from afar.

As they left the mansion, the first rays of dawn breaking over the horizon, they vowed never to speak of what had happened. They hoped to leave the horrors behind them, to start anew. But the shadows seemed to follow them, a dark presence lurking just out of sight.

Lucas and Trey tried to rebuild their lives, but the memory of the mansion and Mark's sacrifice haunted them. They both began to experience strange occurrences: objects moving on their own, whispers in the night, and fleeting glimpses of a shadowy figure.

One evening, as Lucas sat alone in his apartment, he received a call from Trey. "It's happening again," Trey said, his voice trembling. "I can't take it anymore. We need to go back."

"Back? To the mansion?" Lucas asked, a sense of dread washing over him.

"Yes," Trey replied. "We need to find out what happened to Mark. We need to end this, once and for all."

Lucas knew Trey was right. They had to confront the house, to uncover its secrets and put an end to the haunting. They agreed to meet the next morning and make the journey back to the mansion.

Chapter 6
The Return

As they approached the old, ivy-covered building, a sense of foreboding settled over them. The air was thick with the scent of decay and lavender, and the shadows seemed to move with a life of their own.

They entered the mansion, the door creaking ominously as it swung open. The interior was just as they remembered: dark, oppressive, and filled with an eerie silence.

"Eleanora!" Lucas called, his voice echoing through the halls. "We need to talk!"

There was no response. The house seemed empty, abandoned. But Lucas and Trey knew better. They could feel the presence, the malevolent energy that permeated the air.

They made their way to the small, forgotten room at the back of the mansion, where the mirror still stood. Its surface was smooth and clear, reflecting their anxious faces.

"Help us," Lucas whispered, his voice trembling. "We need to know what happened to Mark."

The mirror's surface shimmered, and the voice emerged once more. "Mark is here, bound to the house just as I was. You must free him, as you freed me."

"How?" Trey asked, desperation in his voice.

"There is another ritual," the voice replied. "But it requires a willing soul, someone who will take Mark's place."

Lucas and Trey exchanged a look of horror. They had already sacrificed one of their own. Could they do it again?

But before they could decide, the shadows in the room began to move, coalescing into a dark, humanoid figure. It was Mark, or what was left of him. His eyes were hollow, his expression twisted with pain and anger.

"Lucas, Trey," he whispered, his voice barely audible. "You have to help me. Please."

The sight of Mark, twisted and tormented, filled Lucas and Trey with a sense of urgency. They had to find a way to free him, to end the house's hold on them all. They turned to the mirror, seeking guidance from the voice within.

"The ritual," Lucas said, his voice steady. "Tell us what we need to do."

The voice hesitated, then began to explain. The ritual required a series of steps, each more dangerous than the last. They needed to gather specific items from within the mansion, each imbued with the house's dark energy. Once they had all the items, they would need to perform the ritual in the parlor, where the house's power was strongest.

Lucas and Trey set to work, searching the mansion for the items they needed. The house seemed to resist their efforts, the shadows growing darker and more oppressive. But they pressed on, determined to free Mark and end the haunting.

Their first task was to find the Cursed Locket, a small, silver pendant that had been lost somewhere in the mansion. The voice had warned them that the locket was guarded by a powerful spirit, one of the house's many victims.

They searched room after room, the air growing colder and more oppressive with each step. The whispers grew louder, the shadows darker. Finally, in a dusty old bedroom, they found it. The locket lay on a dresser, its surface tarnished and dull.

As Lucas reached out to pick it up, the temperature in the room plummeted. A figure appeared, a ghostly woman with hollow eyes and a twisted smile. "Leave this place," she hissed, her voice echoing through the room. "Or suffer the same fate as those before you."

Lucas and Trey stood their ground, determined to retrieve the locket. "We just want to free our friend," Lucas said, his voice steady despite the fear gripping his heart.

The ghost's eyes narrowed, and she lunged at them, her form shifting and twisting. Lucas and Trey dodged her attacks, their movements frantic. With a final, desperate grab, Lucas snatched the locket and held it up.

The ghost let out a piercing wail and vanished, the air in the room growing warmer once more. Lucas and Trey exchanged a relieved glance and hurried back to the parlor; the locket clutched tightly in Lucas's hand.

Their next task was to find the Witch's Grimoire, a book of dark spells hidden deep within the mansion's library. The voice had warned them that the book was protected by powerful wards, and they would need to use their wits to retrieve it.

The library was a vast, dusty room filled with rows upon rows of ancient books. Lucas and Trey searched for hours, their eyes straining in the dim light. Finally, they found it. The grimoire lay on a pedestal, its cover adorned with strange symbols.

As they approached, the air crackled with energy, and a barrier of shimmering light appeared around the book. Lucas and Trey racked their brains, trying to remember the spells they had seen Eleanora use.

After several failed attempts, they finally succeeded in breaking the barrier. The grimoire was theirs. They returned to the parlor, the weight of their progress lifting their spirits.

Their final task was to retrieve the Heart of Darkness, a black crystal hidden in the mansion's cellar. The voice had warned them that the cellar was the most dangerous place in the house, filled with dark energy and vengeful spirits.

The cellar was a cold, damp place, the air thick with the scent of decay. Lucas and Trey moved cautiously, their eyes scanning the shadows for any sign of danger. They found the crystal in a small, hidden alcove, its surface pulsing with dark energy.

As they reached for it, the shadows around them came to life, forming into dark, humanoid figures. The spirits attacked, their movements swift and deadly. Lucas and Trey fought back, their determination and desperation giving them strength.

Finally, they retrieved the crystal and fled the cellar, the spirits' wails echoing behind them. They returned to the parlor, their hearts pounding with fear and triumph.

Chapter 8
The Final Sacrifice

With the items gathered, Lucas and Trey knew the final step of the ritual would be the most difficult. They returned to the parlor, their hearts pounding with fear and anticipation.

Eleanora was waiting for them, her expression unreadable. "You have gathered the items," she said, her voice calm. "But the final step requires a willing soul, someone who will take Mark's place."

Lucas and Trey exchanged a look of determination. They knew what they had to do. "We'll do it together," Lucas said, his voice steady. "We'll both take his place."

Eleanora nodded, her eyes filled with a mixture of sorrow and pride. "Very well," she said. "Let us begin."

As Eleanora began the ritual, the air grew thick with energy, the symbols on the floor glowing with a soft, golden light. Lucas and Trey stood side by side, their hands clasped together, their hearts filled with resolve.

The shadows in the room began to writhe and twist, the house's power reaching a fever pitch. The mirror's surface shimmered, and the voice emerged once more. "Thank you," it said, its tone filled with gratitude. "You have freed me. Now, I will help you escape."

Eleanora's chant grew louder, the energy in the room building to a crescendo. The air crackled with power, the shadows growing darker and more oppressive. And then, with a blinding flash of light, it was over.

Chapter 9
The Aftermath

Lucas and Trey found themselves outside the mansion, the morning sun warming their skin. They looked at each other, disbelief and relief mingling in their eyes. They had survived. They were free.

But as they turned to leave, a chilling realization struck them. Eleanora was nowhere to be seen. Had she been consumed by the ritual? Or had she escaped, leaving them to face the house's wrath alone?

The air grew thick with the scent of decay and sulfur, the shadows seeming to follow them as they walked away from the mansion. They knew their ordeal was far from over. The house would continue to haunt them, its malevolent presence a constant reminder of their dark past.

And then, one night, as they slept in their beds, they heard a whisper. A voice they recognized all too well.

"It's not over."

Lucas and Trey awoke with a start, their hearts pounding in their chests. The shadows in their room seemed to move with a life of their own, the air thick with an oppressive energy. They knew the house's hold on them was far from broken.

As they looked at each other, a sense of determination filled their eyes. They had survived the mansion, but their battle was not yet won. They would need to delve deeper into the house's mysteries, to uncover its secrets and put an end to its malevolent power once and for all.

But as they prepared to face the darkness once more, they knew the journey ahead would be long and treacherous. The house would not give up its secrets easily, and the shadows would stop at nothing to claim their souls.

And so, with the weight of their pasts and the hope for a brighter future, Lucas and Trey steeled themselves for the battles to come. The house of secrets would not rest, and neither would they, until they had uncovered the truth and freed themselves from its grasp.

As they gathered their courage and prepared to face the unknown, a chilling realization settled over them. The house's curse was far from broken, and its malevolent power would continue to haunt them until they had paid the ultimate price.

Lucas and Trey knew that they had no choice but to confront the darkness, to face the horrors that awaited them in the depths of the mansion. They would need to uncover the truth about Eleanora, the house, and the dark forces that bound them all.

And so, with a sense of resolve and determination, they set out on their journey, ready to face whatever challenges lay ahead. The house of secrets would not rest, and neither would they, until they had uncovered the truth and freed themselves from its grasp.